Revolution

I0548903

Revolution

MACK REYNOLDS

ÆGYPAN PRESS

This story was first published in the May 1960 issue of *Astounding Science Fiction*.

Special thanks to Greg Weeks, Bruce Albrecht, Stephen Blundell, and the Online Distributed Proofreading Team (which can be found at http://www.pgdp.net).

Mack Reynolds's full true name was Dallas McCord Reynolds.

Revolution
A publication of
ÆGYPAN PRESS
www.aegypan.com

Before you wish for something — or send agents to get it for you — make very, very sure you really want it. You might get it, you know. . . .

Preface

*F*or some forty years critics of the U.S.S.R. have been desiring, predicting, not to mention praying for, its collapse. For twenty of these years the author of this story has vaguely wondered what would replace the collapsed Soviet system. A return to Czarism? Oh, come now! Capitalism as we know it today in the advanced Western countries? It would seem difficult after almost half a century of State ownership and control of the means of production, distribution, communications, education, science. Then what? The question became increasingly interesting following recent visits not only to Moscow and Leningrad but also to various other capital cities of the Soviet complex. A controversial subject? Indeed it is. You can't get much more controversial than this in the world today. But this is science fiction, and here we go.

*P*aul Koslov nodded briefly once or twice as he made his way through the forest of desks. Behind him he caught snatches of tittering voices in whisper.

". . . That's him . . . The Chief's hatchetman . . . Know what they call him in Central America, a *pistola*, that means . . . About Iraq . . . And that time in Egypt . . . Did you notice his eyes . . . How would you like to date *him* . . . That's him. I was at a cocktail party once when he was there. Shivery . . . cold-blooded —"

Paul Koslov grinned inwardly. He hadn't asked for the reputation but it isn't everyone who is a legend before thirty-five. What was it *Newsweek* had called him? "The T. E. Lawrence of the Cold War." The trouble was it wasn't something you could turn off. It had its shortcomings when you found time for some personal life.

He reached the Chief's office, rapped with a knuckle and pushed his way through.

The Chief and a male secretary, who was taking dictation, looked up. The secretary frowned, evidently taken aback by the cavalier entrance, but the Chief said,

"Hello, Paul, come on in. Didn't expect you quite so soon." And to the secretary, "Dickens, that's all."

When Dickens was gone the Chief scowled at his trouble-shooter. "Paul, you're bad for discipline around here. Can't you even knock before you enter? How is Nicaragua?"

Paul Koslov slumped into a leather easy chair and scowled. "I did knock. Most of it's in my report. Nicaragua is . . . tranquil. It'll stay tranquil for a while, too. There isn't so much as a parlor pink —"

"And Lopez — ?"

Paul said slowly, "Last time I saw Raul was in a swamp near Lake Managua. The very last time."

The Chief said hurriedly, "Don't give me the details. I leave details up to you."

"I know," Paul said flatly.

His superior drew a pound can of Sir Walter Raleigh across the desk, selected a briar from a pipe rack and while he was packing in tobacco said, "Paul, do you know what day it is — and what year?"

"It's Tuesday. And 1965."

The bureau chief looked at his disk calendar. "Um-m-m. Today the Seven Year Plan is completed."

Paul snorted.

The Chief said mildly, "Successfully. For all practical purposes, the U.S.S.R. has surpassed us in gross national product."

"That's not the way I understand it."

"Then you make the mistake of believing our propaganda. That's always a mistake, believing your own propaganda. Worse than believing the other man's."

"Our steel capacity is a third again as much as theirs."

"Yes, and currently, what with our readjustment — remember when they used to call them *recessions,* or even earlier, *depressions* — our steel industry is operating at less than sixty percent of capacity. The Soviets always operate at one hundred percent of capacity. They don't have to worry about whether or not they can sell it. If they produce more steel than they immediately need, they use it to build another steel mill."

The Chief shook his head. "As long ago as 1958 they began passing us, product by product. Grain, butter, and timber production, jet aircraft, space flight, and coal —"

Paul leaned forward impatiently. "We put out more than three times as many cars, refrigerators, kitchen stoves, washing machines."

His superior said, "That's the point. While we were putting the product of our steel mills into automobiles and automatic kitchen equipment, they did without these things and put their steel into more steel mills, more railroads, more factories. We leaned back and took it easy, sneered at their progress, talked a lot about our freedom and liberty to our allies and the neutrals and enjoyed our refrigerators and washing machines until they finally passed us."

"You sound like a Tass broadcast from Moscow."

"Um-m-m, I've been trying to," the Chief said. "However, that's still roughly the situation. The fact that you and I personally, and a couple of hundred million Americans, prefer our cars and such to more steel mills, and prefer our personal freedoms and liberties is beside the point. We should have done less laughing seven years ago and more thinking about today. As things stand, give them a few more years at this pace and every neutral nation in the world is going to fall into their laps."

"That's putting it strong, isn't it?"

"Strong?" the Chief growled disgustedly. "That's putting it mildly. Even some of our allies are beginning to waver. Eight years ago, India and China both set out to industrialize themselves. Today, China is the third industrial power of the world. Where's India, about twentieth? Ten years from now China will probably be first. I don't even allow myself to think where she'll be twenty-five years from now."

"The Indians were a bunch of idealistic screwballs."

"That's one of the favorite alibis, isn't it? Actually we, the West, let them down. They couldn't get underway. The Soviets backed China with everything they could toss in."

Paul crossed his legs and leaned back. "It seems to me I've run into this discussion a few hundred times at cocktail parties."

The Chief pulled out a drawer and brought forth a king-size box of kitchen matches. He struck one with a thumbnail and peered through tobacco smoke at Paul Koslov as he lit up.

"The point is that the system the Russkies used when they started their first five-year plan back in 1928, and the system used in China, works. If we, with our traditions of freedom and liberty, like it or not, it works. Every citizen of the country is thrown into the grinding mill to increase production. Everybody," the Chief grinned sourly, "that is, except the party elite, who are running the whole thing. Everybody sacrifices for the sake of the progress of the whole country."

"I know," Paul said. "Give me enough time and I'll find out what this lecture is all about."

The Chief grunted at him. "The Commies are still in power. If they remain in power and continue to develop the way they're going, we'll be through, completely through, in another few years. We'll be so far behind we'll be the world's laughingstock — and everybody else will be on the Soviet bandwagon."

He seemed to switch subjects. "Ever hear of Somerset Maugham?"

"Sure. I've read several of his novels."

"I was thinking of Maugham the British Agent, rather than Maugham the novelist, but it's the same man."

"British agent?"

"Um-m-m. He was sent to Petrograd in 1917 to prevent the Bolshevik revolution. The Germans had sent Lenin and Zinoviev up from Switzerland, where they'd been in exile, by a sealed train in hopes of starting a revolution in Czarist Russia. The point I'm leading to is that in one of his books, 'The Summing Up,' I believe, Maugham mentions in passing that had he got to Petrograd possibly six weeks earlier he thinks he could have done his job successfully."

Paul looked at him blankly. "What could he have done?"

The Chief shrugged. "It was all out war. The British wanted to keep Russia in the allied ranks so as to divert as many German troops as possible from the Western front. The Germans wanted to eliminate the Russians. Maugham had carte blanche. Anything would have gone. Elements of the British fleet to fight the Bolsheviks, unlimited amounts of money for anything he saw fit from bribery to hiring assassins. What would have happened, for instance, if he could have had Lenin and Trotsky killed?"

Paul said suddenly, "What has all this got to do with me?"

"We're giving you the job this time."

"Maugham's job?" Paul didn't get it.

"No, the other one. I don't know who the German was who engineered sending Lenin up to Petrograd, but that's the equivalent of your job." He seemed to go off on another bent. "Did you read Djilas' 'The New Class' about a decade ago?"

"Most of it, as I recall. One of Tito's top men who turned against the Commies and did quite a job of exposing the so-called classless society."

"That's right. I've always been surprised that so few people bothered to wonder how Djilas was able to smuggle his book out of one of Tito's strongest prisons and get it to publishers in the West."

"Never thought of it," Paul agreed. "How could he?"

"Because," the Chief said, knocking the ash from his pipe and replacing it in the rack, "there was and is a very strong underground in all the Communist countries. Not only Yugoslavia, but the Soviet Union as well."

Paul stirred impatiently. "Once again, what's all this got to do with me?"

"They're the ones you're going to work with. The anti-Soviet underground. You've got unlimited leeway. Unlimited support to the extent we can get it to you. Unlimited funds for whatever you find you need them for. Your job is to help the underground start a new Russian Revolution."

*P*aul Koslov, his face still bandaged following plastic surgery, spent a couple of hours in the Rube Goldberg department inspecting the latest gadgets of his trade.

Derek Stevens said, "The Chief sent down a memo to introduce you to this new item. We call it a Tracy."

Paul frowned at the wristwatch, fingered it a moment, held it to his ear. It ticked and the second hand moved. "Tracy?" he said.

Stevens said, "After Dick Tracy. Remember, a few years ago? His wrist two-way radio."

"But this is really a watch," Paul said.

"Sure. Keeps fairly good time, too. However, that's camouflage. It's also a two-way radio. Tight beam from wherever you are to the Chief."

Paul pursed his lips. "The transistor boys are really doing it up brown." He handed the watch back to Derek Stevens. "Show me how it works, Derek."

They spent fifteen minutes on the communications device, then Derek Stevens said, "Here's another item the Chief thought you might want to see:"

It was a compact, short-muzzled handgun. Paul handled it with the ease of long practice. "The grip's clumsy. What's its advantage? I don't particularly like an automatic."

Derek Stevens motioned with his head. "Come into the firing range, Koslov, and we'll give you a demonstration."

Paul shot him a glance from the side of his eyes, then nodded. "Lead on."

In the range, Stevens had a man-size silhouette put up. He stood to one side and said, "Okay, let her go."

Paul stood easily, left hand in pants pocket, brought the gun up and tightened on the trigger. He frowned and pressed again.

He scowled at Derek Stevens. "It's not loaded."

Stevens grunted amusement. "Look at the target. First time you got it right over the heart."

"I'll be . . .," Paul began. He looked down at the weapon in surprise. "Noiseless and recoilless. What caliber is it, Derek, and what's the muzzle velocity?"

"We call it the .38 Noiseless," Stevens said. "It has the punch of that .44 Magnum you're presently carrying."

With a fluid motion Paul Koslov produced the .44 Magnum from the holster under his left shoulder and tossed it to one side. "That's the last time I tote that cannon," he said. He balanced the new gun in his hand in admiration. "Have the front sight taken off for me, Derek, and the fore part of the trigger guard. I need a quick draw gun." He added absently, "How did you know I carried a .44?"

Stevens said, "You're rather famous, Koslov. The Colonel Lawrence of the Cold War. The journalists are kept from getting very much about you, but what they do learn they spread around."

Paul Koslov said flatly, "Why don't you like me, Stevens? In this game I don't appreciate people on our team who don't like me. It's dangerous."

Derek Stevens flushed. "I didn't say I didn't like you."

"You didn't have to."

"It's nothing personal," Stevens said.

Paul Koslov looked at him.

Stevens said, "I don't approve of Americans committing political assassinations."

Paul Koslov grinned wolfishly and without humor. "You'll have a hard time proving that even our cloak and dagger department has ever authorized assassination, Stevens. By the way, I'm not an American."

Derek Stevens was not the type of man whose jaw dropped, but he blinked. "Then what are you?"

"A Russian," Paul snapped. "And look, Stevens, we're busy now, but when you've got some time to do a little thinking, consider the ethics of warfare."

Stevens was flushed again at the tone. "Ethics of warfare?"

"There aren't any," Paul Koslov snapped. "There hasn't been chivalry in war for a long time, and there probably never will be again. Neither side can afford it. And I'm talking about cold war as well as hot." He scowled at the other. "Or did you labor under the illusion that only the Commies had tough operators on their side?"

*P*aul Koslov crossed the Atlantic in a supersonic TU-180 operated by Europa Airways. That in itself galled him. It was bad enough that the Commies had stolen a march on the West with the first jet liner to go into mass production, the TU-104 back in 1957. By the time the United States brought out its first really practical trans-Atlantic jets in 1959 the Russians had come up with the TU-114 which its designer, old Andrei Tupolev named the largest, most efficient and economical aircraft flying.

In civil aircraft they had got ahead and stayed ahead. Subsidized beyond anything the West could or at least would manage, the air lines of the world couldn't afford to operate the slower, smaller and more expensive Western models. One by one, first the neutrals such as India, and then even members of the Western bloc began equipping their air lines with Russian craft.

Paul grunted his disgust at the memory of the strong measures that had to be taken by the government to prevent even some of the American lines from buying Soviet craft at the unbelievably low prices they offered them.

*I*n London he presented a card on which he had added a numbered code in pencil. Handed it over a desk to the British intelligence major.

"I believe I'm expected," Paul said.

The major looked at him, then down at the card. "Just a moment, Mr. Smith. I'll see if his lordship is available. Won't you take a chair?" He left the room.

Paul Koslov strolled over to the window and looked out on the moving lines of pedestrians below. He had first been in London some thirty years ago. So far as he could remember, there were no noticeable changes with the exception of automobile design. He wondered vaguely how long it took to make a noticeable change in the London street scene.

The major reentered the room with a new expression of respect on his face. "His lordship will see you immediately, Mr. Smith."

"Thanks," Paul said. He entered the inner office.

Lord Carrol was attired in civilian clothes which somehow failed to disguise a military quality in his appearance. He indicated a chair next to his desk. "We've been instructed to give you every assistance Mr. . . . Smith. Frankly, I can't imagine of just what this could consist."

Paul said, as he adjusted himself in the chair, "I'm going into the Soviet Union on an important assignment. I'll need as large a team at my disposal as we can manage. You have agents in Russia, of course?" He lifted his eyebrows.

His lordship cleared his throat and his voice went even stiffer. "All major military nations have a certain number of espionage operatives in each other's countries. No matter how peaceful the times, this is standard procedure."

"And these are hardly peaceful times," Paul said dryly. "I'll want a complete list of your Soviet based agents and the necessary information on how to contact them."

Lord Carrol stared at him. Finally sputtered, "Man, *why?* You're not even a British national. This is —"

Paul, held up a hand. "We're co-operating with the Russian underground. Co-operating isn't quite strong enough a word. We're going to *push* them into activity if we can."

The British intelligence head looked down at the card before him. "Mr. Smith," he read. He looked up. "John Smith, I assume."

Paul said, still dryly, "Is there any other?"

Lord Carrol said, "See here, you're really Paul Koslov, aren't you?"

Paul looked at him, said nothing.

Lord Carrol said impatiently, "What you ask is impossible. Our operatives all have their own assignments, their own work. Why do you need them?"

"This is the biggest job ever, overthrowing the Soviet State. We need as many men as we can get on our team. Possibly I won't have to use them but, if I do, I want them available."

The Britisher rapped, "You keep mentioning *our team* but according to the dossier we carry on you, Mr. Koslov, you are neither British nor even a Yankee. And you ask me to turn over our complete Soviet machinery."

Paul came to his feet and leaned over the desk, there was a paleness immediately beneath his ears and along his jaw line. "Listen," he said tightly, "if I'm not on this team, there just is no team. Just a pretense of one. When there's a real team there has to be a certain spirit. A team spirit. I don't care if you're playing cricket, football or international cold war. If there's one thing that's important to me, that I've based my whole life upon, it's this, understand? *I've* got team spirit. Perhaps no one else in the whole West has it, but *I* do."

Inwardly, Lord Carrol was boiling. He snapped, "You're neither British nor American. In other words, you are a mercenary. How do we know that the Russians won't offer you double or triple what the Yankees pay for your services?"

Paul sat down again and looked at his watch. "My time is limited," he said. "I have to leave for Paris this afternoon and be in Bonn tomorrow. I don't care what opinions you might have in regard to my mercenary motives, Lord Carrol. I've just come from Downing Street. I suggest you make a phone call there. At the request of Washington, your government has given me carte blanche in this matter."

*P*aul flew into Moscow in an Aeroflot jet, landing at Vnukovo airport on the outskirts of the city. He entered as an American businessman, a camera importer who was also interested in doing a bit of tourist sight-seeing. He was traveling deluxe category which entitled him to a Zil complete with chauffeur and an interpreter-guide when he had need of one. He was quartered in the Ukrayna, on Dorogomilovskaya Quai, a twenty-eight floor skyscraper with a thousand rooms.

It was Paul's first visit to Moscow but he wasn't particularly thrown off. He kept up with developments and was aware of the fact that as early as the late 1950s, the Russians had begun to lick the problems of ample food, clothing and finally shelter. Even those products once considered sheer luxuries were now in abundant supply. If material things alone had been all that counted, the Soviet man in the street wasn't doing so badly.

He spent the first several days getting the feel of the city and also making his preliminary business calls. He was interested in a new "automated" camera currently being touted by the Russians as the world's best. Fastest lens, foolproof operation, guaranteed for the life of the owner, and retailing for exactly twenty-five dollars.

He was told, as expected, that the factory and distribution point was in Leningrad and given instructions and letters of introduction.

On the fifth day he took the Red Arrow Express to Leningrad and established himself at the Astoria Hotel, 39 Hertzen Street. It was one of the many of the Intourist hotels going back to before the revolution.

He spent the next day allowing his guide to show him the standard tourist sights. The Winter Palace, where the Bolshevik revolution was won when the mutinied cruiser *Aurora* steamed up the river and shelled it. The Hermitage Museum, rivaled only by the Vatican and Louvre. The Alexandrovskaya Column, the world's tallest monolithic stone monument. The modest personal palace of Peter the Great. The Peter and Paul Cathedral. The king-size Kirov Stadium. The Leningrad subway, as much a museum as a system of transportation.

He saw it all, tourist fashion, and wondered inwardly what the Intourist guide would have thought had he known that this was Mr. John Smith's home town.

The day following, he turned his business problem over to the guide. He wanted to meet, let's see now, oh yes, here it is, Leonid Shvernik, of the Mikoyan Camera works. Could it be arranged?

Of course it could be arranged. The guide went into five minutes of oratory on the desire of the Soviet Union to trade with the West, and thus spread everlasting peace.

An interview was arranged for Mr. Smith with Mr. Shvernik for that afternoon.

Mr. Smith met Mr. Shvernik in the latter's office at two and they went through the usual amenities. Mr. Shvernik spoke excellent English so Mr. Smith was able to dismiss his interpreter-guide for the afternoon. When he was gone and they were alone Mr. Shvernik went into his sales talk.

"I can assure you, sir, that not since the Japanese startled the world with their new cameras shortly after the Second War, has any such revolution in design and quality taken place. The Mikoyan is not only the *best* camera produced anywhere, but since our plant is fully automated, we can sell it for a fraction the cost of German, Japanese or American —"

Paul Koslov came to his feet, walked quietly over to one of the pictures hanging on the wall, lifted it, pointed underneath and raised his eyebrows at the other.

Leonid Shvernik leaned back in his chair, shocked.

Paul remained there until at last the other shook his head.

Paul said, in English, "Are you absolutely sure?"

"Yes." Shvernik said. "There are no microphones in here. I absolutely know. Who are you?"

Paul said, "In the movement they call you Georgi, and you're top man in the Leningrad area."

Shvernik's hand came up from under the desk and he pointed a heavy military revolver at his visitor. "Who are you?" he repeated.

Paul ignored the gun. "Someone who knows that you are Georgi," he said "I'm from America. Is there any chance of anybody intruding?"

"Yes, one of my colleagues. Or perhaps a secretary."

"Then I suggest we go to a bar, or some place, for a drink or a cup of coffee or whatever the current Russian equivalent might be."

Shvernik looked at him searchingly. "Yes," he said finally. "There's a place down the street." He began to stick the gun in his waistband, changed his mind and put it back into the desk drawer.

As soon as they were on the open street and out of earshot of other pedestrians, Paul said, "Would you rather I spoke Russian? I have the feeling that we'd draw less attention than if we speak English."

Shvernik said tightly, "Do the Intourist people know you speak Russian? If not, stick to English. Now, how do you know my name? I have no contacts with the Americans."

"I got it through my West German contacts."

The Russian's face registered unsuppressed fury. "Do they ignore the simplest of precautions! Do they reveal me to every source that asks?"

Paul said mildly, "Herr Ludwig is currently under my direction. Your secret is as safe as it has ever been."

The underground leader remained silent for a long moment. "You're an American, eh, and Ludwig told you about me? What do you want now?"

"To help," Paul Koslov said.

"How do you mean, to help? How can you help? I don't know what you're talking about."

"Help in any way you want. Money, printing presses, mimeograph machines, radio transmitters, weapons, manpower in limited amounts, know-how, training, anything you need to help overthrow the Soviet government."

They had reached the restaurant. Leonid Shvernik became the Russian export official. He ushered his customer to a secluded table. Saw him comfortably into his chair.

"Do you actually know anything about cameras?" he asked.

"Yes," Paul said, "we're thorough. I can buy cameras from you and they'll be marketed in the States."

"Good." The waiter was approaching. Shvernik said, "Have you ever eaten caviar Russian style?"

"I don't believe so," Paul said "I'm not very hungry."

"Nothing to do with hunger." Shvernik said. From the waiter he ordered raisin bread, sweet butter, caviar and a carafe of vodka.

The waiter went off for it and Shvernik said, "To what extent are you willing to help us? Money, for instance. What kind of money, rubles, dollars? And how much? A revolutionary movement can always use money."

"Any kind," Paul said flatly, "and any amount."

Shvernik was impressed. He said eagerly, "Any amount within reason, eh?"

Paul looked into his face and said flatly, "Any amount, period. It doesn't have to be particularly reasonable. Our only qualification would be a guarantee it is going into the attempt to overthrow the Soviets — not into private pockets."

The waiter was approaching. Shvernik drew some brochures from his pocket, spread them before Paul Koslov and began to point out with a fountain pen various features of the Mikoyan camera.

The waiter put the order on the table and stood by for a moment for further orders.

Shvernik said, "First you take a sizable portion of vodka, like this." He poured them two jolts. "And drink it down, ah, bottoms up, you Americans say. Then you spread butter on a small slice of raisin bread, and cover it with a liberal portion of caviar. Good? Then you eat your little sandwich and drink another glass of vodka. Then you start all over again."

"I can see it could be fairly easy to get stoned, eating caviar Russian style," Paul laughed.

They went through the procedure and the waiter wandered off.

Paul said, "I can take several days arranging the camera deal with you. Then I can take a tour of the country, supposedly giving it a tourist look-see, but actually making contact with more of your organization. I can then return in the future, supposedly to make further orders. I can assure you, these cameras are going to sell very well in the States. I'll be coming back, time and again — for business reasons. Meanwhile, do you have any members among the interpreter-guides in the local Intourist offices?"

Shvernik nodded. "Yes. And, yes, that would be a good idea. We'll assign Ana Furtseva to you, if we can arrange it. And possibly she can even have a chauffeur assigned you who'll also be one of our people."

That was the first time Paul Koslov heard the name Ana Furtseva.

*I*n the morning Leonid Shvernik came to the hotel in a Mikoyan Camera Works car loaded with cameras and the various accessories that were available for the basic model. He began gushing the advantages of the Mikoyan before they were well out of the hotel.

The last thing he said, as they trailed out of the hotel's portals was, "We'll drive about town, giving you an opportunity to do some snapshots and then possibly to my country dacha where we can have lunch —"

At the car he said, "May I introduce Ana Furtseva, who's been assigned as your guide-interpreter by Intourist for the balance of your stay? Ana, Mr. John Smith."

Paul shook hands.

She was blond as almost all Russian girls are blond, and with the startling blue eyes. A touch chubby, by Western standards, but less so than the Russian average. She had a disturbing pixie touch around the mouth, out of place in a dedicated revolutionist.

The car took off with Shvernik at the wheel. "You're actually going to have to take pictures as we go along. We'll have them developed later at the plant. I've told them that you are potentially a very big order. Possibly they'll try and assign one of my superiors to your account after a day or two. If so, I suggest that you merely insist that you feel I am competent and you would rather continue with me."

"Of course," Paul said. "Now then, how quickly can our assistance to you get underway?"

"The question is," Shvernik said, "just how much you can do in the way of helping our movement. For instance, can you get advanced type weapons to us?"

The .38 Noiseless slid easily into Paul's hands. "Obviously, we can't smuggle sizable military equipment across the border. But here, for instance, is a noiseless, recoilless handgun. We could deliver any reasonable amount within a month."

"Five thousand?" Shvernik asked.

"I think so. You'd have to cover once they got across the border, of course. How well organized are you? If you aren't, possibly we can help there, but not in time to get five thousand guns to you in a month."

Ana was puzzled. "How could you possibly get that number across the Soviet borders?" Her voice had a disturbing Slavic throatiness. It occurred to Paul Koslov that she was one of the most attractive women he had ever met. He was amused. Women had never played a great part in his life. There had never been anyone who had really, basically, appealed. But evidently blood was telling. Here he had to come back to Russia to find such attractiveness.

He said, "The Yugoslavs are comparatively open and smuggling across the Adriatic from Italy, commonplace. We'd bring the things you want in that way. Yugoslavia and Poland are on good terms, currently, with lots of trade. We'd ship them by rail from Yugoslavia to Warsaw. Trade between Poland and U.S.S.R. is on massive scale. Our agents in Warsaw would send on the guns in well concealed shipments. Freight cars aren't searched at the Polish-Russian border. However, your agents would have to pick up the deliveries in Brest or Kobryn, before they got as far as Pinsk."

Ana said, her voice very low, "Visiting in Sweden at the Soviet Embassy in Stockholm is a colonel who is at the head of the Leningrad branch of the KGB department in charge of counter-revolution, as they call it. Can you eliminate him?"

"Is it necessary? Are you sure that if it's done it might not raise such a stink that the KGB might concentrate more attention on you?" Paul didn't like this sort of thing. It seldom accomplished anything.

Ana said, "He knows that both Georgi and I are members of the movement."

Paul Koslov gaped at her. "You mean your position is known to the police?"

Shvernik said, "Thus far he has kept the information to himself. He found out when Ana tried to enlist his services."

Paul's eyes went from one to the other of them in disbelief. "Enlist his services? How do you know he hasn't spilled everything? What do you mean he's kept the information to himself so far?"

Ana said, her voice so low as to be hardly heard, "He's my older brother. I'm his favorite sister. How much longer he will keep our secret I don't know. Under the circumstances, I can think of no answer except that he be eliminated."

It came to Paul Koslov that the team on this side could be just as dedicated as he was to his own particular cause.

He said, "A Colonel Furtseva at the Soviet Embassy in Stockholm. Very well. A Hungarian refugee will probably be best. If he's caught, the reason for the killing won't point in your direction."

"Yes," Ana said, her sensitive mouth twisting. "In fact, Anastas was in Budapest during the suppression there in 1956. He participated."

*T*he dacha of Leonid Shvernik was in the vicinity of Petrodvorets on the Gulf of Finland, about eighteen miles from Leningrad proper. It would have been called a summer bungalow in the States. On the rustic side. Three bedrooms, a moderately large living-dining room, kitchen, bath, even a car port. Paul Koslov took a mild satisfaction in deciding that an American in Shvernik's equivalent job could have afforded more of a place than this.

Shvernik was saying, "I hope it never gets to the point where you have to go on the run. If it does, this house is a center of our activities. At any time you can find clothing here, weapons, money, food. Even a small boat on the waterfront. It would be possible, though difficult, to reach Finland."

"Right," Paul said. "Let's hope there'll never be occasion."

Inside, they sat around a small table, over the inevitable bottle of vodka and cigarettes, and later coffee.

Shvernik said, "Thus far we've rambled around hurriedly on a dozen subjects but now we must become definite."

Paul nodded.

"You come to us and say you represent the West and that you wish to help overthrow the Soviets. Fine. How do we know you do not actually represent the KGB or possibly the MVD?"

Paul said, "I'll have to prove otherwise by actions." He came to his feet and, ignoring Ana, pulled out his shirt tail, unbuttoned the top two buttons of his pants and unbuckled the money belt beneath.

He said, "We have no idea what items you'll be wanting from us in the way of equipment, but as you said earlier all revolutions need money. So here's the equivalent of a hundred thousand American dollars — in rubles, of course." He added apologetically, "The smallness of the amount is due to bulk. Your Soviet money doesn't come in sufficiently high denominations for a single person to carry really large amounts."

He tossed the money belt to the table, rearranged his clothing and returned to his chair.

Shvernik said, "A beginning, but I am still of the opinion that we should not introduce you to any other members of the organization until we have more definite proof of your background."

"That's reasonable," Paul agreed. "Now what else?"

Shvernik scowled at him. "You claim you are an American but you speak as good Russian as I do."

"I was raised in America," Paul said, "but I never became a citizen because of some minor technicality while I was a boy. After I reached adulthood and first began working for the government, it was decided that it might be better, due to my type of specialization, that I continue to remain legally not an American."

"But actually you are Russian?"

"I was born here in Leningrad," Paul said evenly.

Ana leaned forward, "Why then, actually, you're a traitor to Russia."

Paul laughed. "Look who's talking. A leader of the underground."

Ana wasn't amused. "But there is a difference in motivation. I fight to improve my country. You fight for the United States and the West."

"I can't see much difference. We're both trying to overthrow a vicious bureaucracy." He laughed again. "You hate them as much as I do."

"I don't know." She frowned, trying to find words, dropped English and spoke in Russian. "The Communists made mistakes, horrible mistakes and — especially under Stalin — were vicious beyond belief to achieve what they wanted. But they did achieve it. They built our country into the world's strongest."

"If you're so happy with them, why are you trying to eliminate the Commies? You don't make much sense."

She shook her head, as though it was he who made no sense. "They are through now, no longer needed. A hindrance to progress." She hesitated, then, "When I was a student I remember being so impressed by something written by Nehru that I memorized it. He wrote it while in a British jail in 1935. Listen." She closed her eyes and quoted:

"Economic interests shape the political views of groups and classes. Neither reason nor moral considerations override these interests. Individuals may be converted, they may surrender their special privileges, although this is rare enough, but classes and groups do not do so. The attempt to convert a governing and privileged class into forsaking power and giving up its unjust privileges has therefore always so far failed, and there seems to be no reason whatever to hold that it will succeed in the future."

Paul was frowning at her. "What's your point?"

"My point is that the Communists are in the position Nehru speaks of. They're in power and won't let go. The longer they remain in power after their usefulness is over, the more vicious they must become to maintain themselves. Since this is a police state the only way to get them out is through violence. That's why I find myself in the underground. But I am a patriotic Russian!" She turned to him. "Why do *you* hate the Soviets so, Mr. Smith?"

The American agent shrugged. "My grandfather was a member of the minor aristocracy. When the Bolsheviks came to power he joined Wrangel's White Army. When the Crimea fell he was in the rear guard. They shot him."

"That was your grandfather?" Shvernik said.

"Right. However, my own father was a student at the Petrograd University at that time. Left wing inclined, in fact. I think he belonged to Kerensky's Social Democrats. At any rate, in spite of his upper class background he made out all right for a time. In fact he became an instructor and our early life wasn't particularly bad." Paul cleared his throat. "Until the purges in the 1930s. It was decided that my father was a Bukharinist Right Deviationist, whatever that was. They came and got him one night in 1938 and my family never saw him again."

Paul disliked the subject. "To cut it short, when the war came along, my mother was killed in the Nazi bombardment of Leningrad. My brother went into the army and became a lieutenant. He was captured by the Germans when they took Kharkov, along with a hundred thousand or so others of the Red Army. When the Soviets, a couple of years later, pushed back into Poland he was recaptured."

Ana said, "You mean liberated from the Germans?"

"Recaptured, is the better word. The Soviets shot him. It seems that officers of the Red Army aren't allowed to surrender."

Ana said painfully, "How did you escape all this?"

"My father must have seen the handwriting on the wall. I was only five years old when he sent me to London to a cousin. A year later we moved to the States. Actually, I have practically no memories of

Leningrad, very few of my family. However, I am not very fond of the Soviets."

"No," Ana said softly.

Shvernik said, "And what was your father's name?"

"Theodore Koslov."

Shvernik said, "I studied French literature under him."

Ana stiffened in her chair, and her eyes went wide. "Koslov," she said. "You must be Paul Koslov."

Paul poured himself another small vodka. "In my field it is a handicap to have a reputation. I didn't know it had extended to the man in the street on this side of the Iron Curtain."

*I*t was by no means the last trip that Paul Koslov was to make to his underground contacts, nor the last visit to the dacha at Petrodvorets.

In fact, the dacha became the meeting center of the Russian underground with their liaison agent from the West. Through it funneled the problems involved in the logistics of the thing. Spotted through the rest of the vast stretches of the country, Paul had his local agents, American, British, French, West German. But this was the center.

The Mikoyan Camera made a great success in the States. And little wonder. Unknown to the Soviets, the advertising campaign that sold it cost several times the income from the sales. All they saw were the continued orders, the repeated visits of Mr. John Smith to Leningrad on buying trips. Leonid Shvernik was even given a promotion on the strength of his so ably cracking the American market. Ana Furtseva was automatically assigned to Paul as interpreter-guide whenever he appeared in the Soviet Union's second capital.

In fact, when he made his "tourist" jaunts to the Black Sea region, to the Urals, to Turkestan, to Siberia, he was able to have her assigned to the whole trip with him. It gave a tremendous advantage in his work with the other branches of the underground.

Questions, unthought of originally when Paul Koslov had been sent into the U.S.S.R., arose as the movement progressed.

On his third visit to the dacha he said to Shvernik and three others of the organization's leaders who had gathered for the conference, "Look, my immediate superior wants me to find out who is to be your top man, the chief of state of the new regime when Number One and the present hierarchy have been overthrown."

Leonid Shvernik looked at him blankly. By this stage, he, as well as Ana, had become more to Paul than just pawns in the game being played. For some reason, having studied under the older Koslov seemed to give a personal touch that had grown.

Nikolai Kirichenko, a higher-up in the Moscow branch of the underground, looked strangely at Paul then at Shvernik. "What have you told him about the nature of our movement?" he demanded.

Paul said, "What's the matter? All I wanted to know was who was scheduled to be top man."

Shvernik said, "Actually, I suppose we have had little time to discus the nature of the new society we plan. We've been busy working on the overthrow of the Communists. However, I thought . . ."

Paul was uneasy now. Leonid was right. Actually in his association with both Ana and Leonid Shvernik they had seldom mentioned what was to follow the collapse of the Soviets. It suddenly occurred to him how overwhelmingly important this was.

Nikolai Kirichenko, who spoke no English, said in Russian, "See here, we are not an organization attempting to seize power for ourselves."

This was a delicate point, Paul sensed. Revolutions are seldom put over in the name of reaction or even conservatism. Whatever the final product, they are invariably presented as being motivated by liberal idealism and progress.

He said, "I am familiar with the dedication of your organization. I have no desire to underestimate your ideals. However, my question is presented with good intentions and remains unanswered. You aren't anarchists, I know. You expect a responsible government to be in control after the removal of the police state. So I repeat, who is to be your head man?"

"How would we know?" Kirichenko blurted in irritation. "We're working toward a democracy. It's up to the Russian people to elect any officials they may find necessary to govern the country."

Shvernik said, "However, the very idea of a *head man,* as you call him, is opposed to what we have in mind. We aren't looking for a super-leader. We've had enough of leaders. Our experience is that it is too easy for them to become misleaders. If the history of this century has proven anything with its Mussolinis, Hitlers, Stalins, Chiangs, and Maos, it is that the search for a leader to take over the problems of a people is a vain one. The job has to be done by the people themselves."

Paul hadn't wanted to get involved in the internals of their political ideology. It was dangerous ground. For all he knew, there might be wide differences within the ranks of the revolutionary movement. There almost always were. He couldn't take sides. His only interest in all this was the overthrow of the Soviets.

He covered. "Your point is well taken, of course. I understand completely. Oh, and here's one other matter for discussion. These radio transmitters for your underground broadcasts."

It was a subject in which they were particularly interested. The Russians leaned forward.

"Here's the problem," Kirichenko said. "As you know, the Soviet Union consists of fifteen republics. In addition there are seventeen Autonomous Soviet Socialist Republics that coexist within these basic fifteen republics. There are also ten of what we call Autonomous Regions. Largely, each of these political divisions speak different languages and have their own cultural differences."

Paul said, "Then it will be necessary to have transmitters for each of these areas?"

"Even more. Because some are so large that we will find it necessary to have more than one underground station."

Leonid Shvernik said worriedly, "And here is another thing. The KGB has the latest in equipment for spotting the location of an illegal station. Can you do anything about this?"

Paul said, "We'll put our best electronics men to work. The problem as I understand it, is to devise a method of broadcasting that the secret police can't trace."

They looked relieved. "Yes, that is the problem," Kirichenko said.

*H*e brought up the subject some time later when he was alone with Ana. They were strolling along the left bank of the Neva River, paralleling the Admiralty Building, supposedly on a sightseeing tour.

He said, "I was discussing the future government with Leonid and some of the others the other day. I don't think I got a very clear picture of it." He gave her a general rundown of the conversation.

She twisted her mouth characteristically at him. "What did you expect, a return to Czarism? Let me see, who is pretender to the throne these days? Some Grand Duke in Paris, isn't it?"

He laughed with her. "I'm not up on such questions," Paul admitted. "I think I rather pictured a democratic parliamentary government, somewhere between the United States and England."

"Those are governmental forms based on a capitalist society, Paul."

Her hair gleamed in the brightness of the sun and he had to bring his mind back to the conversation.

"Well, yes. But you're overthrowing the Communists. That's the point, isn't it?"

"Not the way you put it. Let's set if I can explain. To begin with, there have only been three bases of government evolved by man . . . I'm going to have to simplify this."

"It isn't my field, but go on," Paul said. She wore less lipstick than you'd expect on an American girl but it went with her freshness.

"The first type of governmental system was based on the family. Your American Indians were a good example. The family, the clan, the tribe. In some cases, like the Iroquois Confederation, a nation of tribes. You were represented in the government according to the family or clan in which you were born."

"Still with you so far," Paul said. She had a very slight dimple in her left cheek. Dimples went best with blondes, Paul decided.

"The next governmental system was based on property. Chattel slavery, feudalism, capitalism. In ancient Athens, for example, those Athenians who owned the property of the City-State, and the slaves with which to work it, also governed the nation. Under feudalism, the nobility owned the country and governed it. The more land a noble owned, the larger his voice in government. I'm speaking broadly, of course."

"Of course," Paul said. He decided that she had more an American type figure than was usual here. He brought his concentration back to the subject. "However, that doesn't apply under capitalism. We have democracy. Everyone votes, not just the owner of property."

Ana was very serious about it. "You mustn't use the words capitalism and democracy interchangeably. You can have capitalism, which is a social system, without having democracy which is a political system. For instance, when Hitler was in power in Germany the government was a dictatorship but the social system was still capitalism."

Then she grinned at him mischievously. "Even in the United States I think you'll find that the people who own a capitalist country run the country. Those who control great wealth have a large say in the running of the political parties, both locally and nationally. Your smaller property owners have a smaller voice in local politics. But how large a lobby does your itinerant harvest worker in Texas have in Washington?"

Paul said, slightly irritated now, "This is a big subject and I don't agree with you. However, I'm not interested now in the government of the United States. I want to know what you people have in store for Russia, if and when you take over."

She shook her head in despair at him. "That's the point the others were trying to make to you. We have no intention of taking over. We don't want to and probably couldn't even if we did want to. What we're advocating is a new type of government based on a new type of representation."

He noticed the faint touch of freckles about her nose, her shoulders — to the extent her dress revealed them — and on her arms. Her skin was fair as only the northern races produce.

Paul said, "All right. Now we get to this third base of government. The first was the family, the second was property. What else is there?"

"In an ultramodern, industrialized society, there is your method of making your livelihood. In the future you will be represented from where you work. From your industry or profession. The parliament, or congress, of the nation would consist of elected members from each branch of production, distribution, communication, education, medicine —"

"Syndicalism," Paul said, "with some touches of Technocracy."

She shrugged. "Your American Technocracy of the 1930s I am not too familiar with, although I understand power came from top to bottom, rather than from bottom to top, democratically. The early syndicalists developed some of the ideas which later thinkers have elaborated upon, I suppose. So many of these terms have become all but meaningless through sloppy use. What in the world does Socialism mean, for instance? According to some, your Roosevelt was a Socialist. Hitler called himself a National Socialist. Mussolini once edited a Socialist paper. Stalin called himself a Socialist and the British currently have a Socialist government — mind you, with a Queen on the throne."

"The advantage of voting from where you work rather than from where you live doesn't come home to me," Paul said.

"Among other things, a person knows the qualifications of the people with whom he works," Ana said, "whether he is a scientist in a laboratory or a technician in an automated factory. But how many people actually know anything about the political candidates for whom they vote?"

"I suppose we could discuss this all day," Paul said. "But what I was getting to is what happens when your outfit takes over here in Leningrad? Does Leonid become local commissar, or head of police, or . . . well, whatever new title you've dreamed up?"

Ana laughed at him, as though he was impossible. "Mr. Koslov, you have a mind hard to penetrate. I keep telling you, we, the revolutionary underground, have no desire to take over and don't think that we could even if we wished. When the Soviets are overthrown by our organization, the new government will assume power. We disappear as an organization. Our job is done. Leonid? I don't know, perhaps his fellow employees at the Mikoyan Camera works will vote him into some office in the plant, if they think him capable enough."

"Well," Paul sighed, "it's your country. I'll stick to the American system." He couldn't take his eyes from the way her lips tucked in at the sides.

Ana said, "How long have you been in love with me, Paul?"

"What?"

She laughed. "Don't be so blank. It would be rather odd, wouldn't it, if two people were in love, and neither of them realized what had happened?"

"Two people in love," he said blankly, unbelievingly.

*L*eonid Shvernik and Paul Koslov were bent over a map of the U.S.S.R. The former pointed out the approximate location of the radio transmitters. "We're not going to use them until the last moment," he said. "Not until the fat is in the fire. Then they will all begin at once. The KGB and MVD won't have time to knock them out."

Paul said, "Things are moving fast. Faster than I had expected. We're putting it over, Leonid."

Shvernik said, "Only because the situation is ripe. It's the way revolutions work."

"How do you mean?" Paul said absently, studying the map.

"Individuals don't put over revolutions. The times do, the conditions apply. Did you know that six months before the Bolshevik revolution took place Lenin wrote that he never expected to live to see the Communist take over in Russia? The thing was that the conditions were there. The Bolsheviks, as few as they were, were practically thrown into power."

"However," Paul said dryly, "it was mighty helpful to have such men as Lenin and Trotsky handy."

Shvernik shrugged. "The times make the men. Your own American Revolution is probably better known to you. Look at the men those times produced. Jefferson, Paine, Madison, Hamilton, Franklin, Adams. And once again, if you had told any of those men, a year before the Declaration of Independence, that a complete revolution was the only solution to the problems that confronted them, they would probably have thought you insane."

It was a new line of thought for Paul Koslov. "Then what does cause a revolution?"

"The need for it. It's not just our few tens of thousands of members of the underground who see the need for overthrowing the Soviet bureaucracy. It's millions of average Russians in every walk of life and every strata, from top to bottom. What does the scientist think when some bureaucrat knowing nothing of his specialty comes into the laboratory and directs his work? What does the engineer in an automobile plant think when some silly politician decides that since cars in capitalist countries have four wheels, that Russia should surpass them by producing a car with five? What does your scholar think when he is told what to study, how to interpret it, and then what to write? What does your worker think when he sees the bureaucrat living in luxury while his wage is a comparatively meager one? What do your young people think in their continual striving for a greater degree of freedom than was possessed by their parents? What does your painter think? Your poet? Your philosopher?"

Shvernik shook his head. "When a nation is ready for revolution, it's the *people* who put it over. Often, the so-called leaders are hard put to run fast enough to say out in front."

*P*aul said, "After it's all over, we'll go back to the States. I know a town up in the Sierras called Grass Valley. Hunting, fishing, mountains, clean air, but still available to cities such as San Francisco where you can go for shopping and for restaurants and entertainment."

She kissed him again.

Paul said, "You know, I've done this sort of work — never on this scale before, of course — ever since I was nineteen. Nineteen, mind you! And this is the first time I've realized I'm tired of it. Fed up to here. I'm nearly thirty-five, Ana, and for the first time I want what a man is expected to want out of life. A woman, a home, children. You've never seen America. You'll love it. You'll like Americans too, especially the kind that live in places like Grass Valley."

Ana laughed softly. "But we're Russians, Paul."

"Eh?"

"Our home and our life should be here. In Russia. The New Russia that we'll have shortly."

He scoffed at her. "Live here when there's California? Ana, Ana, you don't know what living is. Why —"

"But, Paul, I'm a Russian. If the United States is a more pleasant place to live than Russia will be, when we have ended the police state, then it is part of my duty to improve Russia."

It suddenly came to him that she meant it. "But I was thinking, all along, that after this was over we'd be married. I'd be able to show you *my* country."

"And, I don't know why, I was thinking we both expected to be making a life for ourselves here."

They were silent for a long time in mutual misery.

Paul said finally, "This is no time to make detailed plans. We love each other, that should be enough. When it's all over, we'll have the chance to look over each other's way of life. You can visit the States with me."

"And I'll take you on a visit to Armenia. I know a little town in the mountains there which is the most beautiful in the world. We'll spend a week there. A month! Perhaps one day we can build a summer dacha there." She laughed happily. "Why practically everyone lives to be a hundred years old in Armenia."

"Yeah, we'll have to go there sometime," Paul said quietly.

*H*e'd been scheduled to see Leonid that night but at the last moment the other sent Ana to report that an important meeting was to take place. A meeting of underground delegates from all over the country. They were making basic decisions on when to move — but Paul's presence wasn't needed.

He had no feeling of being excluded from something that concerned him. Long ago it had been decided that the less details known by the average man in the movement about Paul's activities, the better it would be. There is always betrayal and there are always counter-revolutionary agents within the ranks of an organization such as this. What was the old Russian proverb? When four men sit down to discuss revolution, three are police spies and the third a fool.

Actually, this had been astonishingly well handled. He had operated for over a year with no signs that the KGB was aware of his activities. Leonid and his fellows were efficient. They had to be. The Commies had been slaughtering anyone who opposed them for forty years now. To survive as a Russian underground you had to be good.

No, it wasn't a feeling of exclusion. Paul Koslov was stretched out on the bed of his king-size Astoria Hotel room, his hands behind his head and staring up at the ceiling. He recapitulated the events of the past months from the time he'd entered the Chief's office in Washington until last night at the dacha with Leonid and Ana.

The whole thing.

And over and over again.

There was a line of worry on his forehead.

He swung his feet to the floor and approached the closet. He selected his most poorly pressed pair of pants, and a coat that mismatched it. He checked the charge in his .38 Noiseless, and replaced the weapon under his left arm. He removed his partial bridge, remembering as he did so how he had lost the teeth in a street fight with some Commie union organizers in Panama, and replaced the porcelain bridge with a typically Russian gleaming steel one. He stuffed a cap into his back pocket, a pair of steel rimmed glasses into an inner pocket, and left the room.

He hurried through the lobby, past the Intourist desk, thankful that it was a slow time of day for tourist activity.

Outside, he walked several blocks to 25th of October Avenue and made a point of losing himself in the crowd. When he was sure that there could be no one behind him, he entered a *pivnaya,* had a glass of beer, and then disappeared into the toilet. There he took off the coat, wrinkled it a bit more, put it back on and also donned the cap and glasses. He removed his tie and thrust it into a side pocket.

He left, in appearance a more or less average workingman of Leningrad, walked to the bus station on Nashimson Volodarski and waited for the next bus to Petrodvorets. He would have preferred the subway, but the line didn't run that far as yet.

The bus took him to within a mile and a half of the dacha, and he walked from there.

By this time Paul was familiar with the security measures taken by Leonid Shvernik and the others. None at all when the dacha wasn't in use for a conference or to hide someone on the lam from the KGB. But at a time like this, there would be three sentries, carefully spotted.

This was Paul's field now. Since the age of nineteen, he told himself wryly. He wondered if there was anyone in the world who could go through a line of sentries as efficiently as he could.

He approached the dacha at the point where the line of pine trees came nearest to it. On his belly he watched for ten minutes before making the final move to the side of the house. He lay up against it, under a bush.

From an inner pocket he brought the spy device he had acquired from Derek Steven's Rube Goldberg department. It looked and was supposed to look considerably like a doctor's stethoscope. He placed it to his ears, pressed the other end to the wall of the house.

Leonid Shvernik was saying, "Becoming killers isn't a pleasant prospect but it was the Soviet who taught us that the end justifies the means. And so ruthless a dictatorship have they established that there is literally no alternative. The only way to remove them is by violence. Happily, so we believe, the violence need extend to only a small number of the very highest of the hierarchy. Once they are eliminated and our transmitters proclaim the new revolution, there should be little further opposition."

Someone sighed deeply — Paul was able to pick up even that.

"Why discuss it further?" somebody whose voice Paul didn't recognize, asked. "Let's get onto other things. These broadcasts of ours have to be the ultimate in the presentation of our program. The assassination of Number One and his immediate supporters is going to react unfavorably at first. We're going to have to present unanswerable arguments if our movement is to sweep the nation as we plan."

A new voice injected, "We've put the best writers in the Soviet Union to work on the scripts. For all practical purposes they are completed."

"We haven't yet decided what to say about the H-Bomb, the missiles, all the endless equipment of war that has accumulated under the Soviets, not to speak of the armies, the ships, the aircraft and all the personnel who man them."

Someone else, it sounded like Nikolai Kirichenko, from Moscow, said. "I'm chairman of the committee on that. It's our opinion that we're going to have to cover that matter in our broadcasts to the people and the only answer is that until the West has agreed to nuclear disarmament, we're going to have to keep our own."

Leonid said, and there was shock in his voice, "But that's one of the most basic reasons for the new revolution, to eliminate this mad arms race, this devoting half the resources of the world to armament."

"Yes, but what can we do? How do we know that the Western powers won't attack? And please remember that it is no longer just the United States that has nuclear weapons. If we lay down our defenses, we are capable of being destroyed by England, France, West Germany, even Turkey or Japan! And consider, too, that the economies of some of the Western powers are based on the production of arms to the point that if such production ended, overnight, depressions would sweep their nations. In short, they can't afford a world without tensions."

"It's a problem for the future to solve," someone else said. "But meanwhile I believe the committee is right. Until it is absolutely proven that we need have no fears about the other nations, we must keep our own strength."

Under his hedge, Paul grimaced, but he was getting what he came for, a discussion of policy, without the restrictions his presence would have put on the conversation.

"Let's deal with a more pleasant subject," a feminine voice said. "Our broadcasts should stress to the people that for the first time in the history of Russia we will be truly in the position to lead the world! For fifty years the Communists attempted to convert nations into adopting their system, and largely they were turned down. Those countries that did become Communist either did so at the point of the Red Army's bayonet or under the stress of complete collapse such as in China. But tomorrow, and the New Russia? Freed from the inadequacy and inefficiency of the bureaucrats who have misruled us, we'll develop a productive machine that will be the envy of the world!" Her voice had all but a fanatical ring.

Someone else chuckled, "If the West thought they had competition from us before, wait until they see the New Russia!"

Paul thought he saw someone, a shadow, at the side of the clearing. His lips thinned and the .38 Noiseless was in his hand magically.

False alarm.

He turned back to the "conversation" inside.

Kirichenko's voice was saying, "It is hard for me not to believe that within a period of a year or so half the countries of the world will follow our example."

"Half!" someone laughed exuberantly. "The world, Comrades! The new system will sweep the world. For the first time in history the world will see what Marx and Engels were *really* driving at!"

*B*ack at the hotel, toward morning, Paul was again stretched out on the bed, hands under his head, his eyes unseeingly staring at the ceiling as he went through his agonizing reappraisal.

There was Ana.

And there was even Leonid Shvernik and some of the others of the underground. As close friends as he had ever made in a life that admittedly hadn't been prone to friendship.

And there was Russia, the country of his birth. Beyond the underground movement, beyond the Soviet regime, beyond the Romanoff Czars. Mother Russia. The land of his parents, his grandparents, the land of his roots.

And, of course, there was the United States and the West. The West which had received him in his hour of stress in his flight from *Mother* Russia. Mother Russia, ha! What kind of a mother had she been to the Koslovs? To his grandfather, his father, his mother and brother? Where would he, Paul, be today had he as a child not been sent fleeing to the West?

And his life work. What of that? Since the age of nineteen, when a normal teenager would have been in school, preparing himself for life. Since nineteen he had been a member of the anti-Soviet team.

A star, too! Paul Koslov, the trouble-shooter, the always reliable, cold, ruthless. Paul Koslov on whom you could always depend to carry the ball.

Anti-Soviet, or anti-Russian?

Why kid himself about his background. It meant nothing. He was an American. He had only the faintest of memories of his family or of the country. Only because people told him so did he know he was a Russian. He was as American as it is possible to get.

What had he told such Westerners, born and bred, as Lord Carrol and Derek Stevens? *If he wasn't a member of the team, there just wasn't a team.*

But then, of course, there was Ana.

Yes, Ana. But what, actually, was there in the future for them? Now that he considered it, could he really picture her sitting in the drug store on Montez Street, Grass Valley, having a banana split?

Ana was Russian. As patriotic a Russian as it was possible to be. As much a dedicated member of the Russian team as it was possible to be. And as a team member, she, like Paul, knew the chances that were involved. You didn't get to be a star by sitting on the bench. She hadn't hesitated, in the clutch, to sacrifice her favorite brother.

*P*aul Koslov propped the Tracy, the wristwatchlike radio before him, placing its back to a book. He made it operative, began to repeat, "Paul calling. Paul calling."

A thin, far away voice said finally, "Okay, Paul. I'm receiving."

Paul Koslov took a deep breath and said, "All right, this is it. In just a few days we're all set to kick off. Understand?"

"I understand, Paul."

"Is it possible that anybody else can be receiving this?"

"Absolutely impossible."

"All right, then this is it. The boys here are going to start their revolution going by knocking off not only Number One, but also Two, Three, Four, Six and Seven of the hierarchy. Number Five is one of theirs."

The thin voice said, "You know I don't want details. They're up to you."

Paul grimaced. "This is why I called. You've got to make — or someone's got to make — one hell of an important decision in the next couple of days. It's not up to me. For once I'm not to be brushed off with that 'don't bother me with details,' routine."

"Decision? What decision? You said everything was all ready to go, didn't you?"

"Look," Paul Koslov said, "remember when you gave me this assignment. When you told me about the Germans sending Lenin up to Petrograd in hopes he'd start a revolution and the British sending Somerset Maugham to try and prevent it?"

"Yes, yes, man. What's that got to do with it?" Even over the long distance, the Chief's voice sounded puzzled.

"Supposedly the Germans were successful, and Maugham failed. But looking back at it a generation later, did the Germans win out by helping bring off the Bolshevik revolution? The Soviets destroyed them for all time as a first-rate power at Stalingrad, twenty-five years afterwards."

The voice from Washington was impatient. "What's your point, Paul?"

"My point is this. When you gave me this assignment, you told me I was in the position of the German who engineered bringing Lenin up to Petrograd to start the Bolsheviks rolling. Are you *sure* that the opposite isn't true? Are you sure it isn't Maugham's job I should have? Let me tell you, Chief, these boys I'm working with now are sharp, they've got more on the ball than these Commie bureaucrats running the country have a dozen times over.

"Chief, this is the decision that has to be made in the next couple of days. Just who do we want eliminated? Are you sure you don't want me to tip off the KGB to this whole conspiracy?"

THE END

www.ingramcontent.com/pod-product-compliance
Lightning Source LLC
Chambersburg PA
CBHW031904170626
46807CB00004B/1887